Ellen: Book Three
THE WAITING
TIME

DOROTHY JOAN HARRIS

ELLEN: BOOK THREE
THE WAITING
TIME

DOROTHY JOAN HARRIS

PENGUIN
CANADA

PENGUIN CANADA

Published by the Penguin Group

Penguin Group (Canada), 90 Eglinton Avenue East, Suite 700, Toronto, Ontario, Canada M4P 2Y3
(a division of Pearson Penguin Canada Inc.)

Penguin Group (USA) Inc., 375 Hudson Street, New York, New York 10014, U.S.A.
Penguin Books Ltd, 80 Strand, London WC2R 0RL, England
Penguin Ireland, 25 St Stephen's Green, Dublin 2, Ireland (a division of Penguin Books Ltd)
Penguin Group (Australia), 250 Camberwell Road, Camberwell, Victoria 3124, Australia
(a division of Pearson Australia Group Pty Ltd)
Penguin Books India Pvt Ltd, 11 Community Centre, Panchsheel Park, New Delhi – 110 017, India
Penguin Group (NZ), cnr Airborne and Rosedale Roads, Albany, Auckland 1310, New Zealand
(a division of Pearson New Zealand Ltd)
Penguin Books (South Africa) (Pty) Ltd, 24 Sturdee Avenue, Rosebank, Johannesburg 2196,
South Africa

Penguin Books Ltd, Registered Offices: 80 Strand, London WC2R 0RL, England

First published 2005

1 2 3 4 5 6 7 8 9 10   (WEB)

LIBRARY AND ARCHIVES CANADA CATALOGUING IN PUBLICATION

Harris, Dorothy Joan, 1931–
Ellen : the waiting time / Dorothy Joan Harris.

(Our Canadian girl)
"Ellen: book three".
ISBN 0-14-305005-2

1. World War, 1939–1945—British Columbia—Vancouver—Juvenile fiction.
2. Poliomyelitis—Juvenile fiction. I. Title. II. Title: Waiting time. III. Series.

PS8565.A6483E447   2005   jC813'.54   C2005-902904-8

Visit the Penguin Group (Canada) website at **www.penguin.ca**

For my Book Club friends:
Suzanne, Jeanie, Carol, and Faye

Yukon

Northwest Territories

Nunavut

British Columbia

Alberta

Saskatchewan

Manitoba

Ont

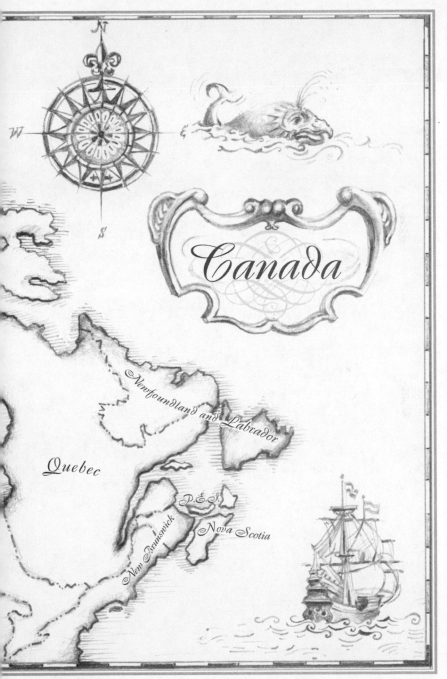

Canada

N
W S

Newfoundland and Labrador

Quebec

P.E.I.

New Brunswick

Nova Scotia

 Marks the location of the story

ELLEN'S STORY CONTINUES

W HEN WE LAST SAW ELLEN, World War II had just begun. Now it is September 1940, and the war has been going on for a year. Food rationing has begun in Canada for such items as meat, butter, sugar, tea, and coffee. Apart from that, the war hasn't affected Ellen very much. Canada is a safe country; its cities are not being bombed. For that reason, some British families have sent their young children to live in Canada, as war guests, until the fighting is over.

But there *is* something frightening going on in Canada and in all of North America—and that is the way that polio is spreading. During the summer many children in Vancouver, and everywhere else, came down with it.

It's hard to remember, now, just how frightening this disease was. Poliomyelitis (sometimes called infantile paralysis) is a virus that spreads easily, especially among children and especially during the hot summer months. Some people who caught polio had mild cases and recovered completely. Others were left paralyzed for life. There isn't a cure for polio, and back in 1940, no one knew how to prevent it. It wasn't until 1954 that Dr. Jonas Salk developed a vaccine against polio that was injected. In 1961, Dr. Albert Sabin developed an oral vaccine as well. After that, everyone in the whole country breathed a huge sigh of relief that the fear of getting polio was over.

Another important thing that people in Ellen's time did not have was an antibiotic. Nowadays, if you get tonsillitis, or any other bad infection, you can get better quite quickly by taking an antibiotic. But in Ellen's time, there were no quick cures, just a long, slow wait until the body could heal itself. And there was no government medical plan either—going to the doctor meant you had a bill to pay, and poor families often couldn't afford that.

We are all so used to telephones today, but in 1940, many families didn't have them. To send an urgent message (when sending a letter would be too slow), you had to send a telegram. And since urgent messages were often bad news, people came to dread seeing a telegram delivery boy knocking at their door—especially if they had fathers or husbands fighting in the war. Unfortunately, many, many telegrams with bad news were sent during World War II. No wonder Ellen is worried at the thought of her father joining the army.

CHAPTER 1

"Oh, dear! Where are the ration books?"
exclaimed Ellen's mother. "I always keep them here in the kitchen drawer."

Ellen looked up from her breakfast porridge. "I haven't touched them, Mum," she said.

"Well, they must be here somewhere," her mother said worriedly, rummaging around in the drawer.

Ellen got up from the table to help her look, and even Grandpa Sanders put down his newspaper. If the ration books were missing, it was a serious matter.

"Maybe they're still in your purse," Ellen suggested. "I'll go get it."

Ellen went off to the big bedroom and came back with her mother's large black purse. Her mother took it and opened it.

"Oh …," she said, her voice weak with relief. "Yes, here they are. I remember now—I was in a hurry to start lunch when I came in on Saturday. That's why I didn't put them away."

Her mother sat down on the nearest chair and put the ration books on the table. Ellen picked up one to look at it. This one was hers, and it had her name on the cover. Inside were pages of little stamps—she'd watched her mother tear one off and give it to the butcher whenever she bought something from him.

"If we didn't have our ration stamps, would that mean we couldn't buy *any* meat or butter?" Ellen asked. "Or tea and coffee and sugar either? Even if we had the money?"

"That's right," said her mother.

Ellen flicked through the pages. The stamps

meant for coffee were all unused, since coffee was too expensive for her family to buy anyway. "But …," she said, in a puzzled tone, "I can understand why sugar and tea and coffee are rationed. Our teacher explained that those things all have to be brought in by ship, and Canada needs all the ships for carrying troops and guns. But why are butter and meat rationed? We have lots of those foods right here in Canada. We don't need ships for them."

"No, but we're sending a lot of food to England. The people there are really short of food because they can't get any supplies from the rest of Europe now."

"Oh. I see," said Ellen, as she put the ration books safely in the drawer and went back to eating her porridge.

It had been more than a year now since the war had started. It hadn't really affected Ellen much so far. In fact, in a way the war had been good for her family: her father had gotten a better job at the factory when the accountant had left to join the army. What affected her most was having to be very quiet while the six o'clock news was on the radio. Her father didn't allow any talking or noise while the news was on.

Although she obeyed that rule, Ellen found it hard to understand just why her parents, and Grandpa Sanders too, got so upset by the war news. After all, Europe was far, far away—a big ocean away, on a different continent. So, lost battles and heavy bombings could hardly affect them here in Vancouver, could they? But Ellen didn't make any remarks like that; she just kept quiet until the news was over.

Now, she finished her porridge and went to gather her school books. Her throat was still sore, she realized. It had been really sore during the night. She wondered whether she should mention it to her mother. But she didn't want to stay home from school—the school year had just started, and she really liked Miss Hillman, her new teacher.

As Ellen gathered her books, she heard a knock at the back door.

"Hi, Amy!" Ellen called out, without even glancing through the back door window. She knew who it would be. Amy Takashima lived next door, and the two girls walked to school together every day. "I'm just coming."

Ellen grabbed a sweater and hurried out to join Amy. The sun was shining brightly and the warm September morning made them both feel like skipping. Ellen decided that her throat wasn't that sore, after all. It was good to be going off to school with her best friend.

"I wonder if Marjorie will be back today," Ellen remarked. "She's been away for days and days."

"Yes," Amy agreed. "She's missed a lot of work already."

Marjorie was their friend, an English girl who had come to Canada. Her parents had been missionaries in China, but the whole family had left to escape the fighting there. She wasn't Ellen's *best* friend, because that was Amy—but still, Ellen hoped that Marjorie would be back soon.

"We could ask Miss Hillman if she knows what's wrong with Marjorie," Amy suggested. "If you're away from school for more than a few days, your parents have to let the school know the reason—otherwise the school sends the truant officer to your house."

"The truant officer? Really?"

"That's what I've heard," said Amy.

"Well," said Ellen, "they'll never have to send the truant officer for me. I like going to school, especially with a nice teacher like Miss Hillman. I wouldn't want to stay home."

When they reached the playground, the girls took a quick look around at the children playing there. But they couldn't see Marjorie anywhere.

And then, in another moment, they knew why. Patsy Greenwood came running up to them, obviously bursting with news.

"You're friends with Marjorie Wells, aren't you?" Patsy asked.

Amy Takashima lived next door, and the two girls walked to school together every day.

"Yes ... why?" said Ellen. "What wrong with her?"

"She has polio!" Patsy exclaimed. Her face showed how pleased she was to be the bearer of such important information.

"*Polio*? How do you know that?" Ellen demanded.

"I know because my father's a doctor and he told me," said Patsy.

Ellen and Amy looked at each other in horror. "Polio?" Ellen whispered again.

The radio broadcasts and the newspapers had been full of stories all summer about polio: how it was a virus that spread quickly in the hot weather and how it seemed to strike mostly children. There were stories, too, about how the authorities were trying to keep the virus from spreading by closing the public swimming pools and cancelling any Saturday matinees for children at the movies. The stories explained that polio usually started like a bad case of flu—but it was much, much worse than flu. Those who got a bad case of it were sometimes left paralyzed. Ellen had seen pictures in the newspaper of children who were now in wheelchairs because they'd had polio.

And now their friend had it?

CHAPTER N°. 2

Patsy was going on.

"My father says Marjorie may have caught it by going to the Pacific National Exhibition last month. He wouldn't let me go this year, because there are always crowds there. He says where there are crowds, there are lots of germs, and he doesn't want me near anybody's germs. Did your parents let you go?"

Ellen shook her head. She didn't say that she didn't have the money to go on rides or buy cotton candy anyway. Amy didn't answer either. They were both still stunned by the news.

"Is … is Marjorie paralyzed?" Ellen managed to ask.

"I don't know," said Patsy. "My father didn't tell me that."

When they went into their classroom, though, Ellen got an answer to her question.

"I've received a note from Marjorie's mother," Miss Hillman told the class. "Marjorie has been sick with polio, but luckily it was a fairly mild case, and she's home from the hospital now. So I thought it would cheer her up if we all wrote a letter to her."

So it *was* true, Ellen thought. A *mild* case of polio, Miss Hillman had said. What was a mild case?

Miss Hillman was holding up a big sheet of paper with "GET WELL SOON!" written in capital letters across the top. Row by row, everyone in the class went up to Miss Hillman's desk and wrote something on the big sheet. Ellen's row was the last to go up. By then she could see that almost everyone had written the same thing: "Get well soon."

Ellen thought fast. She wanted to say something more to Marjorie. In her best writing she wrote, "I wish you were back at school. I miss you. Do you miss us? Love, Ellen."

When everyone had finished, Miss Hillman asked, "Now, who knows where Marjorie lives and can take this letter to her?"

Quickly, Ellen put up her hand.

"Oh, thank you, Ellen," said Miss Hillman with a grateful smile. "I'll give it to you when you leave after school."

Ellen was pleased to get one of Miss Hillman's smiles. But then she heard Patsy whispering something to the girl beside her—and her good feeling disappeared. "I wouldn't go to her house," Patsy was saying. "I'll bet you can catch polio just by breathing the same air as a sick person!"

Was that true? Ellen wondered. The thought preyed on her mind all day. And when, after school, she and Amy set off home with the rolled-up sheet of paper, Amy said much the same thing.

"Um … I don't think I should go with you," Amy said slowly. "My mother has been telling me all summer that I wasn't to go near anyone who is sick. So I'd better go straight home."

"Oh," said Ellen. Now her worried feeling grew. Her own mother had been giving her the same warning, Ellen realized. "Oh," she said again. "But—I promised Miss Hillman that I'd take it."

She watched as Amy headed home. By now, Ellen was wishing that she hadn't put up her hand so quickly—even if it had earned her a smile from Miss Hillman. But then she thought, too, of Marjorie, who was her friend. Ellen knew that if *she* were sick in bed, she would like to have a letter like this. After all, she didn't have to go inside Marjorie's house.

Ellen walked, more slowly now, down the block and around the corner to Marjorie's house. She knocked on the door, and when Marjorie's mother opened it, Ellen held out the rolled-up letter.

"This is for Marjorie," she said. "Our teacher sent it."

"Did she? Well, thank you," said Mrs. Wells.

"It's from all the class. We all wrote in it," Ellen explained. Then she went on—because she just *had* to ask. "Is Marjorie para—" Ellen cut off the word. "I mean, can she still walk?"

Mrs. Wells gave a big sigh. "Yes. Yes, she can. And we're very thankful for that. All our church was praying for her. But one leg is weak, she'll need a brace on it." Mrs. Wells held the door open wider. "Won't you come in and visit for a while? She's been so lonely."

"Uh … well, I have to get home—" Ellen began.

"Just for a moment then," Mrs. Wells urged. She held out her hand to draw Ellen in. "She hasn't seen any of her friends for so long."

Ellen didn't know what to do then. It would sound so rude to say that she wasn't allowed to go in. But she really was afraid to now.

As if reading her thoughts, Mrs. Wells said, "Just come in for a moment. The doctors have said that Marjorie is not contagious now. You could just stand in the doorway and talk to her."

Ellen let herself be drawn inside and down the hallway to Marjorie's room. From the doorway, she could see Marjorie lying in bed. Ellen was shocked at how white and thin her friend looked.

"Here's Ellen to see you, Marjorie," Mrs. Wells was saying. She was making her voice sound cheerful, Ellen could tell. "She's brought something for you from your teacher."

"It's from all of us," Ellen explained. "We all wrote something for you. We hope you'll be better soon."

Marjorie lifted herself up to see the letter her mother was holding out. "Oh, thank you," she said. "But tell me what's going on at school. Is our teacher nice? Is my desk still there?"

Marjorie sounded so eager to hear any news that Ellen couldn't help staying—still standing in the doorway—and talking to her for a while. And when she left, she even promised Marjorie that she'd come again soon.

And then she ran all the rest of the way home, so that her mother wouldn't ask why she was late.

From the doorway, she
could see Marjorie lying
in bed. Ellen was shocked
at how white and thin
her friend looked.

At supper, Ellen's throat felt really sore again, sore enough that it hurt to swallow. Her mother noticed her pushing her food around her plate.

"Aren't you hungry, Ellen?" her mother asked.

"Not really," said Ellen. "And my throat's sore. It hurts to swallow."

"Your throat is sore?"

Her mother's voice, which was usually quite soft, rose to a sudden sharp pitch. Ellen looked up, surprised. Then her mother got up from her chair and came to put her hand on Ellen's forehead.

"Oh, dear. She does feel hot," she said to Ellen's father.

Ellen was even more surprised to see that her father and Grandpa Sanders had both stopped eating and were staring at her. Her father got up too and came to feel her forehead.

"Yes, she certainly has a fever," he said. "You'd better take her to the doctor tomorrow. First thing in the morning."

"To the doctor?" said Ellen. She was really startled now. "But—it costs a lot to go the doctor, doesn't it? I've had sore throats before. Why do I have to go to the doctor?"

Ellen's mother looked at her for a moment before answering.

"Because …," she said slowly, "a sore throat and fever are the first symptoms of polio."

Ellen stared back at her mother, wide-eyed, too stunned to speak. It couldn't be. It just couldn't be.

"You haven't gone anywhere there were crowds, have you, Ellen?" her father was asking. "Or been around anyone sick? Is there anybody at school who has it?"

Ellen nodded, still too overcome to speak. "Marjorie's had it," she whispered. "She's been away for ages. But she's much better now." Ellen didn't mention how she knew this last bit.

"Well—you can leave your supper if it hurts too much to swallow," her mother told her. "Maybe something hot to drink would be better. You go make up your bed and lie down, and I'll bring it to you."

All this concern made Ellen even more uneasy. She was never allowed to waste food by leaving her supper uneaten. And to be told to go lie down instead of helping with the dishes as she always did—that was more worrying than anything.

Ellen went to the living room and spread her bedclothes out on the chesterfield. Since the house had only two bedrooms, Ellen's bed was the chesterfield. She'd been sleeping there for so long that she was quite used to it. It had been a year and a half since her father had lost his job at the bank and they'd had to give up their own house and move in, all three of them, with Grandpa Sanders. Even now, after her father had found an office job again, they were still there in Grandpa Sanders's small house. When they'd first moved there, Ellen had said to herself every night, *I wish I still had a room of my own.* She didn't say that every night any more. Just sometimes.

Tonight, her only thought was *I wish I were all better.* And also *I wish I hadn't gone to Marjorie's house.* She didn't want to have to tell her mother about that. But then—her sore throat had started long *before* she'd gone to Marjorie's. So she couldn't have caught it there, could she?

Ellen lay on the chesterfield, looking out at the streetlight, with fearful thoughts filling her mind. She couldn't stop thinking about the newspaper photographs of children in wheelchairs. Even worse was remembering one photo of a girl whose breathing had been affected. She had to lie in a huge contraption called an iron lung that pushed the air into and out of her lungs to keep them working. If the bellows on the iron lung stopped working, so would her breathing.

Later, after everyone else was asleep, Ellen lay in the dark for a long time, breathing in and breathing out and listening to her breath. She thought about what it would be like not to be able to do that, not to be able to breathe on her own.

The more she thought about it, the harder it became to breathe until she could almost *feel* that big iron lung closing in around her in the dark.

CHAPTER N°. 4

Ellen hadn't thought she would ever sleep that night. But she did—and she awoke in the morning to find her mother bending over her.

"How do you feel?" she asked anxiously, putting her hand on Ellen's forehead. "Is your neck stiff? Can you get up?"

Ellen was awake in a second. All her bad dreams came flooding back. She pushed her bedclothes aside and struggled to her feet.

"Of course I can get up," she said.

Her mother gave her a tiny smile. "Good," she said. "Then come and try to eat a little breakfast.

I've made Cream of Wheat cereal for you—that will be easier to swallow than porridge."

At breakfast, everyone was very silent. Even Grandpa Sanders, who was apt to talk on and on about how the war was going, even he was quiet.

Her father did break the silence to ask, "You'll take the bus, won't you?"

"Oh, yes," answered her mother.

And that, in itself, was unexpected. Usually they all walked everywhere—to work, to church, to school, to shop. The bus fare was eight cents, and now that Ellen was almost eleven and getting taller, she had to pay adult fares. So getting to the doctor's and home again would cost thirty-two cents, without counting what the doctor's bill would be.

Ellen and her mother set out right after breakfast. Even so, when they reached the clinic, there were several other people waiting. As they sat in the waiting room, Ellen tried to keep her mind off her sore throat by studying the posters on the walls.

There was one poster that urged everyone to save rubber, glass, paper, and rags because they could all be turned in and used for the war effort.

There was another poster urging people to buy war bonds. At school, there were war bonds for children to buy, Ellen knew—you brought in a quarter every week and bought a stamp to put in a booklet. Sixteen stamps, or four dollars, filled the booklet, and after the war was over, you could turn it in and the government would pay you five dollars.

Then there was another poster that said "Join the armed forces now. Your country needs YOU!" The poster had a picture of a soldier pointing right out at her. The soldier had fair hair and a thin face; Ellen thought he looked a bit like her father—

"The doctor will see you now."

The nurse's voice interrupted Ellen's thoughts. She got up and followed her mother into the doctor's office.

Though the doctor had a kindly face and greeted them both pleasantly, Ellen's heart was pounding with fear. Her mother explained why they were there, and then the doctor spent quite a few minutes looking into her throat, getting her to say "Aah," and feeling her neck and behind her ears.

Finally, Ellen couldn't wait another second. "Is it—do I have polio?" she blurted out. "Please tell me!"

"Polio?" The doctor looked down at her anxious face. "No," he said, right away. "It's not polio. It's tonsillitis. I can see that your tonsils are quite inflamed."

"So ... so I won't end up in an iron lung?" Ellen asked.

"No," he said again, smiling sympathetically. "Is that what you were worrying about?"

"We were all worried," said Ellen's mother. "Because of Ellen having a sore throat and fever, you see."

The doctor nodded. "There have certainly been a lot of polio cases this summer. But this sore throat is from enlarged tonsils. Just keep her in bed, give her lots to drink and some Aspirin for the fever. If the tonsillitis keeps coming back, then later on she might need an operation to remove her tonsils."

The doctor talked to Ellen's mother awhile longer, but once Ellen had heard the words "It's not polio," she scarcely listened to anything more. She felt limp with relief. It wasn't until they were on the bus going home that she remembered the doctor's mention of an operation.

"An operation to take out my tonsils would cost a lot, wouldn't it?" she asked her mother. "More than just going to a doctor?"

"Well … yes," her mother agreed. "*If* it's ever needed."

That's all right then, thought Ellen. *If an operation costs a lot, we wouldn't have the money for it anyway. So I won't worry about that.*

*The doctor spent quite a few
minutes looking into her
throat, getting her to say
"Aah," and feeling her neck
and behind her ears.*

When they were home again, and Ellen had changed back into her nightgown, she got another small surprise.

"Since you're supposed to stay in bed," her mother said, "you'd better settle down in our bed during the day."

The big double bed was a much more comfortable place to be, Ellen found. Lying there, reading her library book and not being asked to help with any housework, was an unexpected way to spend a day. But with her throat hurting so badly, it was hard to really enjoy it.

"My throat feels as if it's on fire," she told her mother.

"Well, I gave you an Aspirin when we got home," her mother said. "I don't think I can give you any more just now."

Ellen sighed. "I wish there were something magical to take the hurt away."

Her mother shook her head. "No, there's nothing like that, I'm afraid. It will just take time to get better."

"How much time?"

"We'll have to wait and see. I'll bring you something hot to drink."

Her mother was being very sympathetic, Ellen realized. Even Grandpa Sanders had nothing disapproving to say about her lying in bed all day. And just after four o'clock, there was a knock at the back door.

It was Mrs. Takashima.

"Amy say I must come," she said to Ellen's mother. "She want to know why Ellen not at school."

Amy's voice floated up from the bottom of the back steps. "Mum wouldn't let me come in case it was polio," she said. "But it *isn't,* is it?"

"No, it's not," Ellen's mother told them. "It's tonsillitis. Ellen just has to stay in bed and rest."

Hearing this, Ellen got out of bed and came to stand in the bedroom doorway. "I'm okay," she called out, in a croaky voice.

"Oh, good!" Amy had come up the back steps and was peeking around her mother. "Patsy was telling us all that you probably had polio now, because you went to Marjorie's house with that card from the class."

Ellen's mother turned and looked sharply at Ellen. "You went to Marjorie's?"

"Just to give her mother the card that the class had made," Ellen explained, not quite truthfully. "But, Mum—my throat was sore *long* before that."

"Oh." Her mother's look softened a bit. "Well—you'd better get back into bed now."

"I'll tell everybody at school what you have," Amy called out. "I'm glad you're not paralyzed or anything."

A little later, Ellen's father came hurrying in.

"Goodness—you're home early!" her mother exclaimed.

"I know. I left work early. I just had to know if Ellen was all right."

"Yes, it's just tonsillitis," said her mother, with a happy smile. "She has to rest in bed, so she's in our room."

Ellen's father gave a big sigh of relief and hurried

into the bedroom. "I was worrying about you all day," he told her. Then he turned to her mother. "Maybe we should think about getting a telephone in the house. You could have phoned me at work as soon as you got home from the doctor."

"Yes, I could have," her mother agreed. "But I don't know anybody on the street with a telephone. The Takashimas don't have one."

"I should think not! Telephones cost a lot!" This outburst was from Grandpa Sanders, who had appeared in the doorway. "Why, you have to pay a bill for your telephone every month, whether you use it or not! There'll be no telephones in this house."

Her father made no reply to that. But to Ellen's surprise, he bent down then and gave her a big hug. "I'm glad you're going to be all right," he said, his voice breaking a bit.

Ellen was really surprised by the big hug. They were not the sort of family who did much hugging or kissing. But being hugged like that by her father did feel so good.

CHAPTER 5

That night, back on the chesterfield, Ellen lay awake for a long time. She was feverish, she knew—her skin felt hot. Looking out at the streetlight again, she thought back to how scared she had felt last night. And she had been even more scared sitting in the clinic waiting room, looking at the posters there.

But then, the image from one of those posters rose in her mind—the one that said "Your country needs YOU." The one with the soldier who looked a bit like her father.

What if ... what if her father saw one of those

posters and decided to join the armed forces? Grandpa Sanders was always talking about *his* days as a soldier in what he called the Great War, the one that started back in 1914. And talking, too, about how any strong young man should be glad to serve his country. Did her father feel that way?

Here was a whole new worry for Ellen. She didn't want her father to go off and join the army. Or the navy, like Will. Will was a man who had done odd jobs for them the summer before, while he was out of work—he'd joined the navy, and he wrote to them every month or two. But her father wasn't out of work, not any more. He had a good job again, in the factory office.

Ellen tried not to think about this possibility; she tried to think about something else. But the picture of her father in a uniform, walking away from them, down a platform toward a troop train, kept creeping into her mind. And when at last she did sleep, her dreams were feverish and confused, full of soldiers and trains and people crying.

The next morning, as soon as her father came to the breakfast table, Ellen just had to ask about it. "Dad," she began, "what does your factory make? Is it something important?"

"Well, it's important to us," he answered. "It pays my salary."

"I mean … is it important to the war?"

"Not directly. Though the ball-bearings and chains that we make are used in a lot of machines."

That didn't really tell Ellen what she wanted to know. All day, as she lay in the big bed, her worry kept nagging at her mind. And to her dismay, at suppertime Grandpa Sanders started in again, about how the war wasn't going well, more troops were needed, and all young men should be joining up.

To everyone's surprise, Ellen burst into tears.

"Ellen! What's wrong?" said her mother. "Is your throat worse?"

Ellen shook her head. "No," she managed to say. "It's not that. But I don't want Dad to join up. I don't want him to go away—"

"Oh, Ellen," said her father, "have you been worrying about that?'

Ellen nodded. "There was this poster in the doctor's clinic. It said 'Your country needs YOU.' And the soldier in the poster looked a bit like you."

Her father smiled, a little sadly, and took off his glasses. "The army would never take me," he said, showing her the thick lenses on his glasses. "Not with my weak eyes."

"Really?" said Ellen. "Really and truly?"

"Really and truly," said her father. "Here—take my hanky and wipe your eyes." He handed her a big handkerchief and gave her a fond look. "I'm glad that you would miss me," he added.

"Miss you! Of course I would," said Ellen.

Ellen dried her eyes and tried to swallow some of her supper, while Grandpa Sanders found a new subject to talk about—the shocking way that the war was causing prices to rise. He went on about that for quite a while. After supper, Ellen's father didn't go right back to his chair and newspaper.

"I have a little errand to run," he said as he went out the back door.

In a few minutes, he was back with a small paper bag. He was smiling.

"I went to the corner store and bought us a brick of ice cream," he said. "I thought that would feel good on a sore throat."

Ellen's eyes lit up. Ice cream was a real treat.

"Oh, thank you, Dad," said Ellen. "What kind is it?"

"Neapolitan. The kind you like."

The brick of ice cream, sliced in four, made a serving for each of them. Ice cream always had to be eaten up right away, since they had no way to keep it frozen.

"You're spoiling the girl," grumbled Grandpa Sanders. "You're not going to waste twenty-five cents on ice cream every night, are you?"

"No, not every night," said Ellen's father. "It's a little celebration."

Grandpa Sanders didn't ask what they were celebrating. But Ellen thought she knew.

CHAPTER No 6

"*Ellen, do you think you would be all*
right without me this afternoon?"

It was the next morning. Her mother was
smoothing out the sheets on the big bed so that
Ellen could lie there. "Grandpa Sanders will be
here, of course," her mother went on, "but he
usually sleeps after lunch."

"Sure, I'll be fine," said Ellen. "But where are
you going?"

"It's my afternoon to go to the Women's
Group at the church," said her mother. "We all
want to do something for the war effort, so we

roll bandages for the Red Cross. And we're filling ditty bags too, to send to sailors."

"Ditty bags? What a funny name," said Ellen. "What are they?"

Her mother smiled. "I guess it is a strange name. But the sailors are glad of them. They're bags that we fill with the warm socks and scarves we've all been knitting," she explained. "And we put in things like toothpaste and shaving soap and writing paper—all sorts of things that sailors might need when they're at sea for weeks at a time."

"Do you think Will has maybe gotten one of those bags?" asked Ellen.

"He might have."

"We haven't heard from him for a long time."

"No, but if he's at sea, he can hardly post a letter." Her mother paused as a thought struck her. "Maybe you'd like to knit something for the ditty bags, while you're home like this. I could bring some wool for you from the supplies at the church."

"Okay," said Ellen. "I'm not very good at knitting, but I could do a scarf."

When her mother came home that afternoon, she gave Ellen several large balls of wool, all of them dark grey.

"Is that what I'm to use?" said Ellen. "It's not a very pretty colour."

"Sailors don't want pretty colours," said her mother. "They just need something warm. It gets really cold at sea, especially on the night watches."

As well as the wool, Ellen's mother had brought home some old magazines that one of the women had left at the church.

"I thought you might like to look at these," she told Ellen.

There weren't usually any magazines in their house—magazines cost money—and Ellen took them eagerly. They were mostly copies of a magazine called *The Canadian Home Journal*, with articles about homemaking, along with lots of recipes and a few stories.

The recipes didn't interest her—especially ones that told how you could make cakes without using much sugar or how to stretch your one pound of rationed meat and make a dish that would feed a big family. The stories were better, even if they were about grown-ups. But it was the colourful advertisements all through the magazines that fascinated Ellen.

What a life you could live in the houses from these photographs, Ellen thought. There were telephones in every house, of course, shiny black ones sitting on elegant desks. There were vacuum cleaners that could suck up dirt from rugs right on the floor—no more taking rugs outside to shake the dust out of them. There were kitchens with shiny white electric stoves and shiny white counters and shiny tiled floors. There were pictures of refrigerators, big ones as tall as a person, with a freezing compartment where you could keep things like ice cream. Imagine being able to have ice cream right in your house, Ellen marvelled, so you could have some whenever you wanted! There was even one advertisement for an electric dishwasher, showing dishes stacked in a rack inside a cabinet. But Ellen figured that was too far-fetched—how could a machine possibly wash dishes without breaking them?

Still, it was wonderful to dream about living in houses like these.

The next day Ellen's mother cast on the stitches for her and Ellen got started on knitting a scarf for a sailor's ditty bag. She worked at it all morning. And that very day a letter arrived.

"Look, Ellen," said her mother. "Here's a letter from Will at last."

It was the usual strange-looking letter—no envelope, just the paper he'd written on stuck together at the edges. And, as usual, Will didn't say a lot in his letter.

He started with "Well, folks, I hope your all OK and thanks for your letters. I haven't bin able to write for a while. We were forty-eight days at sea this time."

He went on to say how cold it was at sea, how boring the night watches could be, and how tired they got of eating nothing but tinned food. He said he'd sure like some of the apples he used to pick when he had found work in the Okanagan, and he said how much they all looked forward to getting into port again.

Ellen looked up from reading. "Will doesn't write very well, does he?" she said. "He says *your* instead of *you're*. And he makes some spelling mistakes too."

"That's true," said her mother. "But remember—he grew up on the prairies. Children who lived on farms often had so much work to do at home that they didn't have time for school. And if he lived away out in the country, there might not even have been a school close enough for him to walk to."

"He doesn't tell us what port they're in," Ellen pointed out.

"No, sailors mustn't say anything like that, anything about the ship's movements. Otherwise the censor would black it out."

"The censor?" Ellen exclaimed. "You mean somebody reads all their letters and censors them? What if they've written something really personal? Really private?"

Her mother smiled. "I'm sure the censors are used to that. They only black out information about where ships are heading and that sort of thing."

Ellen looked at the letter again. Then she had a new thought. "Does the censor read *our* letters too?" she asked.

"No," said her mother, "there's nothing we could say that could help the enemy."

"I guess not," Ellen agreed.

Ellen kept the letter beside her as she went back to her knitting. She tried to imagine what it would be like to be at sea for weeks at a time. Knitting was pretty boring, but it was less boring when she let herself imagine being on a ship, on a cold night, or let herself picture some sailor with her scarf muffled around his neck. It was easier to keep on knitting with pictures like that in her mind.

"When *am I going to feel better?*" Ellen asked, some days later, her voice still croaky. "It's been days and days since we went to the doctor, and my throat still hurts."

"I know," said her mother.

"Isn't there *anything* you can do?"

"No. You just have to wait for your tonsils to heal."

"I've been waiting for days already," Ellen complained.

"You had some Aspirin this morning," said her mother. "Did that help?"

48

"Only a bit. I wish there were some magic medicine that would cure my tonsils right away. I don't want to wait any longer. I want to be all better and go back to school and see my friends."

"Well, your friend Marjorie has been sick for a lot longer than you have, and she's still waiting to get all well," her mother pointed out.

That was true, Ellen had to admit. But somehow, knowing someone else was worse off than she was didn't make her feel any less miserable. She felt as if her throat had been hurting forever. And she'd quite forgotten about being grateful that she didn't have polio.

Before she'd gotten sick, the thought of being allowed to just lie in bed and read all day would have sounded wonderful. But it wasn't wonderful. It was lonely. And because she sometimes dozed in the comfort of the big bed, she often lay awake at night, which was lonelier still. It was too easy to think gloomy thoughts, lying awake when everyone else was asleep.

Sometimes Ellen would prop herself up on

the chesterfield in the morning and look out, to watch the other children going past on their way to school. She wanted to be going with them, off to play in the playground, to skip, even to do spelling and arithmetic. Just to be with her friends.

"I wish I could go back to school," she would whisper to herself day after day. "I wish I could go to the library. I wish Amy could come and keep me company."

Amy had come to the back door several times to ask how Ellen was. But she was not allowed to come in and visit with Ellen. After the alarming number of new polio cases there'd been that summer, Amy's mother, like Ellen's mother, was very nervous about any kind of germs.

Today, though, was different.

When Amy came to the back door about four o'clock, she had a big smile on her face.

"My mother's friend, Mrs. Kogawa, explained to her what tonsillitis was," she announced. "She told my mum that if I didn't go too close and didn't touch anything of yours, I'd be all right. So I can come in and visit today."

"Oh, that's great!" cried Ellen, who had heard all this from the bedroom. "Come on in. Isn't that great, Mum?"

"Yes, it is," her mother agreed, moving a chair into the bedroom doorway for Amy. "Only not too much talking, Ellen. Your voice is still croaky."

"But I can listen just fine," Ellen pointed out. "I'm so glad to see you, Amy. I've finished my library books and I've been so bored."

"Well," said Amy, setting some papers down on the bed, "you may not be so glad to have these. Miss Hillman has sent a lot of arithmetic for you to do so that you don't get too far behind."

"I don't even mind doing arithmetic," Ellen told her. "Now—sit down and tell me everything that's been going on in the class."

"Everything? Well, I'll try," said Amy. "First of all, we have a new boy in the class called Anthony. He's English, he talks like Marjorie does, and Miss Hillman told us he's a war guest."

"A war guest?" said Ellen.

"Yes. His parents sent him to live with his aunt here in Vancouver. His parents figure he'll be safer here in Canada, now that London is being bombed every night by the Germans."

"Did he live in London? Has his house been bombed?'

"He didn't say if his house has been bombed already or if it just might be soon. He doesn't talk much. I think he's lonely, being away from his parents and so far from his home."

"I guess he would be," Ellen said. "I know I would be."

"And then Patsy has been telling us all about her birthday party last weekend. She had balloons and party hats and a cake shaped like a heart, all decorated with icing roses, and everybody at the party got a present to take home as a party favour."

"A present to take *home*?" said Ellen. "I thought you took presents *to* a birthday party."

"Well, that's what you do at a fashionable birthday party, Patsy says—give every guest a party favour to take home. Mary had been invited to the party and she was wearing her favour today, a pretty glass necklace."

Ellen thought briefly of her own birthday, which was coming up soon. She'd be eleven, but *she* wouldn't be having any party like that. She might not even be getting a present this year, not with having to pay the doctor's bill and all.

"Some people have all the luck, don't they?" she said, rather wistfully.

But Amy just shrugged. "We don't celebrate birthdays that much," she explained. "Japanese families celebrate Girls' Day, on the third of March. In Japanese, it's *Hina matsuri*. It's really a doll festival. My mother gets out her little ceremonial Japanese dolls, and she makes special lucky cookies with bean curd in them. I like those better than birthday cake anyway."

After Amy had gone, promising to return soon, Ellen looked carefully through the papers her friend had brought. She was secretly hoping she might find a card from all the class among the arithmetic papers—like the one they'd made for Marjorie. And she had wanted to ask Amy if Miss Hillman was planning to make one.

Maybe … maybe you had to have something really serious, like polio, to get a class card. It would've been nice though.

Ellen's mother allowed her to get out of bed to have her meals at the table. That was less messy than eating in bed. But Ellen didn't have a dressing gown, and it felt strange to sit at the table in her faded nightgown, even with her mother's cardigan buttoned around her.

Her mother was being very kind, Ellen realized, bringing her hot drinks when she was in bed and making special custards that were easy to swallow. And her father kept urging her to eat.

"You're getting thin, Ellen," he would say. "Try to eat a little more."

Ellen didn't think she looked any different, but she did notice how wobbly her legs were whenever she got out of bed.

In the evenings, she was allowed to sit in the living room to listen to her favourite radio programs. Sometimes, when she was really bored, she even looked at the newspaper that her father and Grandpa Sanders read so avidly.

Today, the newspaper had a big photograph on the front page. It was of a house in London that had been bombed—the front half of the house had been sliced off cleanly so that you stared right in at the bedroom upstairs and the kitchen below. It looked rather like a doll's house with its front taken off. Only it wasn't a doll's house; it was somebody's home. Maybe even Anthony's, or somebody like him. It must have been a child's bedroom, because there was a pair of bunny slippers under the bed. And down in the kitchen there was a teapot on the table, not even broken.

Ellen looked around their own living room and tried to imagine it with the front wall blown off. Where would they go? Where would the owner of those slippers be sleeping now? Or had she been killed by the bomb that had hit her house?

Once more, Ellen found herself lying awake that night, staring at the streetlight. She hadn't realized that ordinary people like her got hurt in war. It wasn't just soldiers and sailors who got killed, but children wearing bunny slippers. And was Anthony lying awake, she wondered, missing his mother? When she did get to sleep, her dreams were vivid, full of houses being sliced apart. She was glad to wake up.

All these nights of lying awake were changing her, Ellen realized. *Is this what growing up means,* she thought, *feeling other people's pain?*

If it was, she figured she'd rather go back to being a child.

CHAPTER No 8

Ellen's mother usually shopped several mornings a week, since she could carry only one or two bags home from the store at a time. This day she was a lot longer getting home.

"What kept you?" Grandpa Sanders asked, as soon as she came in the door. "I'm getting hungry for my lunch."

"Oh, I had an extra stop to make," said her mother, dropping the bags on the kitchen counter.

"What were you buying?" said Grandpa Sanders suspiciously. He didn't like to see money being spent on anything unnecessary.

"I didn't buy anything," Ellen's mother answered. "I went to the library."

"The library?" Ellen called from the bedroom. "Really? Did you get me some books?"

Her mother was smiling at her eagerness. "Yes, I went to the children's section and I saw some old favourites that *I* used to read. So I picked one out for you."

Her mother handed over a book and Ellen pounced on it. It was called *The Secret Garden*.

"That was my favourite book when I was your age," her mother said. "I used to try to read it at school, with the book hidden on my lap. I got into trouble for that, I remember."

"Did you?" Ellen stared at her mother in surprise. It was hard to picture her mother getting into trouble.

"I think I'll read it again when you've finished it," her mother said now.

Ellen started right in on the book, and soon she was caught up in the story of cross, lonely Mary, who wandered unhappily around her uncle's big estate until she came upon the small locked garden.

With something new to read, the afternoon flew by. Ellen read all afternoon and all evening, until nine o'clock. She wanted to stay up and read some more. But nine o'clock was when Grandpa Sanders wanted all the lights out in the house, to save on electrical bills. He had always insisted on that, and now he could say that saving electricity was a patriotic duty as well.

So tonight, as Ellen lay on the chesterfield, her thoughts weren't gloomy. They were full of Mary and poor lame Colin. And that made her think of Marjorie too. Mrs. Wells had said that Marjorie would need a brace on her weak leg. Maybe *she* could help Marjorie, the way Mary had helped Colin in the book. Ellen wanted to picture herself doing something to help Marjorie—but she wasn't sure just what. Pushing Marjorie in a wheelchair would certainly be a helpful thing to do. Only—Marjorie wasn't going to be in a wheelchair, according to what Mrs. Wells had said. So, Ellen wondered, what *could* she do?

By the next afternoon, Ellen had finished the book. She was sorry to finish it—she was always sorry when she'd finished a really good book. She lay back on her pillow, just thinking about it. And then a new thought struck her—since she didn't have anything more to read, maybe she could *write* a story.

Not like that book, of course—she lived in Vancouver, not Yorkshire, and there were no locked gardens in these small backyards. But a story about herself and Marjorie. She'd have to find some paper to write on, which might be a problem. But then she remembered a half-empty notebook from last year that she'd tucked away in a drawer.

Ellen hopped out of bed and went to her drawer. Yes, there was at least half of the notebook unused. She got a pencil from the kitchen and settled down to write. Now what would she call the girls in her story? Marjorie could be Margaret, perhaps, and for herself—perhaps Judith Anne … or Sarah Jane. Ellen was such a *plain* name.

Ellen chewed on her pencil and thought hard.
Now what could she have the girls do? What
exactly could *she* do for Marjorie? Ellen thought
about this for a long time without writing more
than the first paragraph.

Writing a story was harder than Ellen had
expected it to be.

She stared at the empty ruled pages for a while
longer. *Maybe I could at least write a letter to Marjorie,*
Ellen thought. *If I asked her, Mum might take it
over to Marjorie's house.*

Ellen tore out a page from the notebook and
started to write. She had lots to tell Marjorie,
especially about being sick too. She knew now
how lonely and bored Marjorie must be. Even
more lonely and bored than she was, because
Marjorie had been much sicker and had been
home much longer.

Ellen ended up filling three pages from the
notebook. Her father saw them on the bed when
he got home that night.

"What have you been writing?" he asked.

"I tried writing a story but I couldn't think of anything to say, so I wrote a letter to Marjorie instead. She's the one who has polio. Only … I can't exactly take it over to her."

"No," her father agreed. "But I could take it on my way to work tomorrow, if you tell me where she lives."

"Oh, Dad—would you?" said Ellen.

"Humph!" said Grandpa Sanders. "You spoil that girl."

CHAPTER No 9

The calendar in the kitchen had been turned to October just a few days after Ellen had gotten sick. From her place at the kitchen table Ellen could see it every morning as the days crawled past. After the first week, she'd taken to marking the days off with a cross, but the crosses seemed to mount up so slowly. Was that what sailors stuck on a ship did? And was Marjorie doing this too? *As soon as I'm better, I'll visit her,* she thought. *I promise I will. Marjorie doesn't even have Amy coming in.*

Not that Amy came in every day—she had to

practise her piano pieces a lot for a recital that was coming up. But she came in when she could. And today was a day she could.

"More homework from Miss Hillman," Amy announced as she came in. "We're doing long division now."

Ellen pulled a face—though in truth she was glad of some work to do. "Thanks," she said. "I'll have to get my dad to help me with that."

"How do you feel now?" Amy asked. "Are you getting better?"

"Well, a bit better … though my throat is still sore. Mum says I have to be patient. But I just can't *wait* to get back to school and see everybody again."

"Yes, it's hard to be patient," Amy said sympathetically. "*I* can't wait until this recital is over, so I don't have to practise all the time."

"And I can't wait till I can get dressed again," Ellen went on. "I'm so tired of wearing these old nighties."

"And at recess today, Anthony was saying *he*

can't wait till he's old enough to join the air force and start shooting down the planes that are bombing London. He says when he gets a bit taller, he's going to lie about his age and join up."

"Really?" said Ellen. "What's he like, this Anthony?"

"Well, he's quite tall already," said Amy. "He got into a fight one recess time. He was fighting Herbie, who's in Grade Seven and a lot bigger, because Herbie said that England was losing the war."

"Did Anthony get into trouble?"

"No, when the principal heard what they were fighting about, it was Herbie who got into trouble. The principal made Herbie write out all the words to 'There'll Always Be an England.'"

"Oh. And what else is going on in the class?" asked Ellen.

"Let me see … Well, Patsy has a new plaid skirt, pleated all around—only you mustn't call it 'plaid,' she says. It's a Scottish tartan. It's her family's own pattern."

"Do families have their own private patterns of material?" asked Ellen.

"She says real Scottish families do. And she says her parents are going to let her take lessons in Scottish dancing."

"I'd like to have a pleated skirt one day," Ellen said wistfully, "one that flares out when you twirl around. Patsy sure has nice clothes."

"She sure does," Amy agreed.

One day Mrs. Takashima came in too, with a plate of special cookies. "These special good luck cookies," she told Ellen. "Usually only for New Year. But I make for you to bring you good luck."

The cookies were shaped like cherry blossoms, and they were filled with a sweet paste that Amy said was bean curd. Ellen thanked her very politely for bringing them. But later, when she'd tried one, she didn't like the taste very much.

"Still, it was kind of Amy's mother to bring them," Ellen told her mother.

Her mother had been taking Ellen's temperature every morning as soon as she awoke. But this morning, when her mother looked at the thermometer she frowned and looked at it more closely.

"What's wrong?" Ellen asked.

"Your temperature is up," her mother said, with a worried expression. "Let's take it again."

The second reading was just as high.

"Ellen, you haven't been doing anything you shouldn't, have you?" her mother asked.

"You know I haven't, Mum," Ellen answered. "How could I, when I haven't been out of the house for weeks?"

But her mother's frown didn't go away, and Ellen could hear her telling the bad news to Ellen's father.

"You'll have to check with the doctor," her father said in reply, "and ask him what we should do. Perhaps you could go to the Johnsons' house—they have a telephone now. I'm sure if you explained, they'd let you use their telephone to call the clinic."

"Do you think … do you think this means Ellen will have to have her tonsils out now?" her mother said nervously.

"I don't know," said her father. "Maybe it does mean that."

Ellen, overhearing all this from her place on the chesterfield, felt her heart sink. *An operation?* she whispered to herself. She'd have to have an operation after all?

Ellen didn't eat much breakfast. Neither did her mother. And as soon as her mother thought the clinic would be open, she put on her coat to go down the street to the Johnsons' house.

Ellen waited anxiously for her to come back. She tried to do some of the arithmetic Amy had brought, but she couldn't concentrate on anything. At last she heard her mother's step on the back porch.

"What did the doctor say?" Ellen called out, as soon as her mother opened the door. "Do I have to have an operation?"

"No ... not right now, anyway," her mother said. "The doctor told me to give you more Aspirin, and lots and lots to drink, to see if that brings down your temperature. He doesn't want to take your tonsils out unless it's really necessary. He said that not all doctors agree, but *he* believes that tonsils can help screen out germs, maybe even the polio virus. So for now, we just wait."

More waiting, thought Ellen. Still, she was glad that that was what the doctor advised. Ellen dutifully swallowed the Aspirin and didn't complain when her mother kept bringing her more and more glasses of water to drink.

By evening, her temperature was down again. And it stayed that way the next day as well. The worried frown left her mother's face and Ellen's fearful imaginings stopped.

More days went by. But then, on a fine Saturday morning, Ellen realized something.

"It doesn't hurt to swallow any more!" she exclaimed. "My sore throat is gone!"

"Really?" said her mother. "Your throat isn't sore at all?"

"Not a bit," said Ellen. "And my temperature has been normal for days now. So does this mean I can go back to school?"

"Well, perhaps. Let's see how you are tomorrow."

"But if I'm fine tomorrow, can I go to school on Monday?" Ellen asked eagerly.

"Perhaps. But you'll have to dress warmly," her mother warned. "It's a lot colder now, you know."

CHAPTER N° 10

How strange it was to be outside again! To be walking to school with Amy and seeing all the other children streaming toward the school! The leaves had been falling from the trees while she was sick, Ellen realized—there were piles of leaves on the sidewalks to scuff through. And everyone was wearing warm jackets now, not just sweaters. To her dismay, Ellen's mother had insisted that she dress warmly and wear the long brown stockings that Ellen hated. So, no more knee socks until springtime now, she thought sadly.

Still, it was wonderful to be heading back to school, wonderful to see her friends again, wonderful to have Miss Hillman say, "Welcome back, Ellen. We've missed you."

It was all wonderful, until Gwen, who sat at the desk in front of Ellen, refused to sit down.

"My mother says I'm not to go near anybody with germs," she said.

Ellen just stared at Gwen. She could feel her face turning red. "But—I'm all better now," she stammered. "And besides, it was tonsillitis I had, not polio."

Everyone in the class was staring at Ellen and Gwen now. The room was very quiet. Miss Hillman put down the piece of chalk she was holding and turned to face the whole class.

"Now I want you all to listen to me," Miss Hillman began. "I know you, and your parents too, have been worried about catching polio this past summer. But there have been no new cases of polio in Vancouver for weeks now. And what's more, Ellen is right, Gwen—tonsillitis isn't catching in the same way polio is."

Ellen darted an angry glance at Gwen and started to breathe a little easier.

Miss Hillman was going on. "As you know, Marjorie *has* had polio. Luckily, it was not too bad a case, though she will probably need a brace on one leg. But, and this is important," she said firmly, "she is over the polio now, so when she comes back to school, you must not make her feel uncomfortable." Miss Hillman looked solemnly at all the class. "I want you to promise that."

Everyone in the class looked solemn too, as they all nodded their heads. And Gwen, after a little hesitation, took her seat in front of Ellen.

"Now, let's all take out our arithmetic notebooks and get to work," Miss Hillman said.

Ellen was glad to settle into her arithmetic and try to forget about Gwen. But at recess, it was another matter. When Ellen walked over to where the girls were skipping, Gwen turned to face her.

"I don't care what Miss Hillman says. I don't want you skipping with us," Gwen announced. "And it's *my* skipping rope."

Again, Ellen felt her face go red. The two girls holding the rope looked a bit sheepish, but they didn't urge Gwen to change her mind.

Ellen turned and walked away, over to where Amy and another girl were playing jacks. Would they tell her to go away too? Ellen wondered. But they obviously hadn't heard Gwen's outburst and made no objection to Ellen joining them.

During noon hour and afternoon recess, Ellen avoided Gwen on the playground. And since she wasn't used to being up all day, Ellen began to feel too tired to care about skipping anyway.

The next day, there was some more whispering from Gwen and her friends when Ellen arrived at school. But, surprisingly, it was Patsy who spoke up.

"You're just being silly, Gwen," Patsy said. "My father says we can't catch anything from Ellen now—and he knows, because he's a doctor.'

I don't want you skipping with us," Gwen announced. "And it's my skipping rope.

Ellen just stared for a moment. Then she smiled. "Thanks, Patsy," she said.

Patsy had another surprise when they got to the classroom. She went up to Miss Hillman with a letter in her hand. Ellen recognized it as the kind of letter without an envelope that Will usually sent.

"My big brother is in the navy," she told Miss Hillman importantly. "He's a lieutenant, and he wrote a letter just for me."

"Would you like to read it to the class?" said Miss Hillman.

Patsy stood at the front and started to read. It was an interesting letter. Her brother described what it was like to stand at the bow of the ship at night and see bright streaks in the waves, streaks that were caused by the phosphorus in the ocean. He described how dolphins liked to play in the bow waves of the ship, how they would keep up with the ship and leap through the waves it made. He told about the seagulls that followed the ship, even far out at sea, waiting for the cook to throw the garbage over the stern. He wrote about how silent it was on night watches and how bright the stars were out there on the ocean, far from any city lights.

Then Patsy showed how one line had been blacked out.

"That's what the censor does," Patsy told the class. "He checks to see if there's anything that might help the enemy and blacks it out."

"But you're not the enemy," someone in the class objected.

"No, but the letter might be seen by somebody else," Patsy explained.

"What do you think it said? If you hold it up to the light can you tell?"

"No, I tried that already," said Patsy, holding the letter up. "See? It's blacked out too heavily to see anything."

There were a few more questions from the class, and then Miss Hillman said, "Well, thank you, Patsy, for bringing in such an interesting letter. Your brother must have a great imagination," she added with a smile.

Ellen sat at her desk, thinking that *she'd* had a letter from a sailor too. But would she want to read Will's letter out to the class, with all the mistakes? Would she get interested questions from the class … and a smile from Miss Hillman?

Ellen wasn't at all sure about that.

By the next day, Ellen was feeling less tired. After school, she decided to keep her promise to herself—she would go to visit Marjorie. Amy had to hurry home for her piano lesson, but Ellen turned at the corner that led to Marjorie's street.

It seemed so long ago that she'd last climbed these steps to Marjorie's front door. It *was* weeks ago, of course, but it seemed even longer—Ellen felt like a different person somehow. Those weeks of lying in bed, and especially of lying awake at night, had changed her. Now she found herself thinking about what *other* people were feeling. And compared with Marjorie, or Anthony, or the child in the bombed house, Ellen felt very lucky.

Mrs. Wells was pleased to see her, and Marjorie was even more pleased.

"Oh … you're back at school!" Marjorie exclaimed. "I wish I could go. I got your letter, but I haven't seen anybody. So tell me everything that's happening."

"Well, I've only been back at school for three days myself—but I'll tell you what I can," said Ellen.

She was careful not to say anything about Gwen not wanting to sit near her and not letting her join in the skipping. Ellen wondered what Gwen would say if she found out that Ellen had actually gone inside Marjorie's house. *She would probably refuse to sit by me again!* Ellen thought. And she suspected that Gwen would give

Marjorie a hard time when she came back to school, in spite of what Miss Hillman had said. So *she* would have to be an especially good friend to Marjorie then—she *knew* how awful it felt to be shunned by others.

Ellen didn't stay long with Marjorie; she knew her mother would be wondering where she was. And even though she hurried the rest of the way home, her mother did ask why she was late. "I saw Amy get home at least fifteen minutes ago," her mother said.

"I stopped to say hello to Marjorie," Ellen explained.

"To Marjorie?" Her mother frowned at that.

"It's all right, Mum," Ellen said. "She's not a bit contagious now. And she hasn't had anybody visit her all these weeks."

Her mother pursed her lips, but didn't say anything more.

The kitchen calendar had been turned to November now. Ellen looked at the square for Saturday—the 4th and her birthday. Would her parents remember? Usually, Ellen herself would put a big circle around the date. But she hadn't done that this year. They still had the doctor's bill to pay, she knew, so there might not be any presents this year.

That night, as they all sat listening to the radio at six o'clock, the news was especially bad. A Canadian ship had gone down in the Atlantic Ocean.

"Would all the sailors have drowned?" Ellen whispered to her mother.

"Perhaps not," her mother whispered back. "If the ship was in a convoy, then some of them might have been rescued."

The news announcer didn't give the name of the ship, Ellen noticed. But there would be telegrams being delivered to a lot of homes, she knew—those dreaded telegrams that started with "The Minister of Defence deeply regrets to inform you …" She had sometimes seen telegram boys, on their bicycles, pedalling around the streets. Since most people didn't have telephones, urgent news of any kind usually came in a telegram. How awful it would be, if you had a father in the navy, to get a telegram just now. You'd be afraid to open it … and yet you'd know that you had to. Ellen thought of Will, too, and how happy he had looked when they last saw him, and she wondered if his family was getting one of those telegrams.

Oh, why do there have to be wars? she whispered to herself. Then she remembered Will's letter. She *would* take it in and read it to the class, she decided. After all, how would he feel if he thought she were ashamed of him, just because he'd never gotten the chance to learn how to spell properly? *Even if he can't write a long interesting letter, like Patsy's brother,* she told herself, *he's working just as hard to win the war.*

On Saturday morning, Ellen was still asleep when her mother and father came into the living room.

"Happy birthday, Ellen!" they said together. "Happy eleventh birthday!"

Ellen was awake in an instant. They *had* remembered! And there *was* a present to unwrap—a pretty quilted dressing gown and new slippers.

"You won't have to wear my cardigan over your nightgown any more," said her mother. "Not that we want you to be sick again!" she added.

Even Grandpa Sanders, looking a little embarrassed, gave her something. "Here's a quarter for you," he said gruffly. "Put it in your piggy bank and save it for something useful."

Since it was Saturday, there were cleaning chores to be done. And now that Ellen was well again, she had to help, of course. As she sprinkled the wet tea leaves from their breakfast tea onto the living room rug, to keep the dust down while she swept it, she thought of the vacuum cleaners in the magazine advertisements. Would they ever have one of those to use? What she would like best from the wonderful things in those advertisements, she decided, was a telephone. Why, with one of those in the house you'd never have to feel lonely. She and Marjorie could have talked to each other every day, all the while they were both sick. They could even have helped each other with their homework. Yes, a telephone would be a wonderful thing. But Ellen doubted that her family would ever have one.

At lunchtime, there were more surprises.

There was a birthday cake, which her mother had been keeping hidden in the oven. She took it out of its hiding place with a great flourish. "I made it yesterday while you were at school," she told Ellen.

There was ice cream ("Ice cream *again*?" said Grandpa Sanders) and Amy had been invited to come for lunch. Amy brought a present too: a small red lacquer dish to put on a dresser and keep hair pins in. "I know you don't have a dresser right now," said Amy, "but maybe you will one day."

When the candles on the cake were being lit, Ellen's mother told her, "Don't forget to make a wish."

Ellen thought quickly. She could wish for a room of her own—she'd wished for that last year. Or she could wish for a twirly pleated skirt … or for really good marks at school so that Miss Hillman would praise her …

"Come on—blow!" said her mother. "The candles are burning down."

A room of my own, Ellen wished and blew.

"All the candles out with one blow," said her father. "That means your wish will come true."

Will it? Ellen wondered. *Will it really? Then maybe I should have wished for something more important …*

"And you get another wish when you cut the first piece of cake, you know," her father reminded her.

"Oh—yes. I'd forgotten that," said Ellen. So, this time, she closed her eyes and wished hard. *I wish that the war would be over very soon,* she said to herself.

After Amy had gone home, Ellen helped her mother with the dishes. It actually felt good, she realized, to be able to do that again. And as they stood there at the sink, Ellen decided to be honest with her mother.

"Mum," she began, "Marjorie is going to need a brace on her leg for a while. So she'll need help getting to school. And I want to help her. I'll have to leave earlier in the morning, but I really want to do this."

Ellen's mother turned and looked at her for a long moment.

"She doesn't have polio any more," Ellen said firmly. "She's my friend, Mum. And *I* can walk just fine."

Her mother was silent for a moment longer. Then she nodded.

"Yes. All right," she said. "I think you should do that."

And to Ellen's surprise, her mother took her hands out of the dishwater and gave her a big soapy hug. And Ellen hugged her back.

Dear Reader,

Welcome back to Our Canadian Girl! In addition to this story about Ellen, there are many more adventures of other spirited girls to come.

So please keep on reading. And do stay in touch. You can also log on to our website at www.ourcanadiangirl.ca and enjoy fun activities, sample chapters, a fan club, and monthly contests.

Sincerely,
Barbara Berson
Editor

1608
Samuel de
Champlain
establishes
the first
fortified
trading post
at Quebec.

1759
The British
defeat the
French in
the Battle
of the
Plains of
Abraham.

1812
The United
States
declares war
against
Canada.

1845
The expedition of
Sir John Franklin
to the Arctic ends
when the ship is
frozen in the pack
ice; the fate of its
crew remains a
mystery.

1869
Louis Riel
leads his
Métis
followers in
the Red
River
Rebellion.

1871
British
Columbia
joins
Canada.

1755
The British
expel the
entire French
population
of Acadia
(today's
Maritime
provinces),
sending
them into
exile.

1776
The 13
Colonies
revolt
against
Britain, and
the Loyalists
flee to
Canada.

1762
Elizabeth

1837
Calling for
responsible
government, the
Patriotes, following
Louis-Joseph
Papineau, rebel in
Lower Canada;
William Lyon
Mackenzie leads the
uprising in Upper
Canada.

1867
New
Brunswick,
Nova Scotia
and the United
Province of
Canada come
together in
Confederation
to form the
Dominion of
Canada.

1870
Manitoba joins
Canada. The
Northwest
Territories
become an
official
territory of
Canada.

Timeline

1885
At Craigellachie, British Columbia, the last spike is driven to complete the building of the Canadian Pacific Railway.

1898
The Yukon Territory becomes an official territory of Canada.

1914
Britain declares war on Germany, and Canada, because of its ties to Britain, is at war too.

1918
As a result of the Wartime Elections Act, the women of Canada are given the right to vote in federal elections.

1945
World War II ends conclusively with the dropping of atomic bombs on Hiroshima and Nagasaki.

1873
Prince Edward Island joins Canada.

1896
Gold is discovered on Bonanza Creek, a tributary of the Klondike River.

1905
Alberta and Saskatchewan join Canada.

1917
In the Halifax harbour, two ships collide, causing an explosion that leaves more than 1,600 dead and 9,000 injured.

1939
Canada declares war on Germany seven days after war is declared by Britain and France.

1949
Newfoundland, under the leadership of Joey Smallwood, joins Canada.

1897
Emily

1885
Marie-Claire

1940
Ellen